THE GIRL WHO LOVED PURPLE

Written by
Priscilla Doremus

Illustrated by
Ariane Elsammak

The Girl who Loved Purple
Copyright © 2022, Priscilla Joy Doremus

priscilladoremus.com

SEVEN BEARS
PUBLISHING

Illustration: Arianne Elsammak, artbyari.com

Publishing Services: Melinda Martin, MartinPublishingServices.com

ISBN: 978-1-7361474-8-1 (paperback), 978-1-7361474-9-8 (case laminate)

Printed in China

For anyone who has
ever loved purple.

Once upon a lilac day,
Early in the month of May,
Pippa went outside to play
In the grassy meadow.

"I love purple!" she declared,
When at lavender she stared.
Plucked it up and some she shared
With her dearest mother.

Mother bought her purple clothes,
Rows and rows of purple bows.
From her head down to her toes—
Pippa wore some purple.

As time passed, she loved it more,
In each shade and from each store.
"Mother dear, I just adore
Every shade of purple!"

"Other colors I don't like.
I won't ride an orange bike!
Blue jump ropes might work for Mike,
But mine must be purple!"

When her birthday rolled around,
Queen of Purple she was crowned
Gifts of purple to astound,
Except from her friend, John.
John's gift wasn't purple, no.
He brought her a red yo-yo.
Thought that she would love it so—
Just as much as he did.

Pippa didn't like the gift.
"It's not purple!" she said, miffed.
Mother's eyes now made the shift
To her purple princess.

"Pippa, you are out of line
Thinking purple so divine.
Do you think purple so fine—
Finer than John's friendship?"

"Mother, it's the greatest thing!
It makes my heart dance and sing.
I would give up EVERYTHING
Just to get more purple."

That night as she went to bed,
Mother came to kiss her head.
Pondering what Pippa said,
Mother told this story.

"Once upon a violet night,
When the stars shine bold and bright,
One star shone with special light,
Telling of a baby.

This baby was like no one.
Perfect, flawless, God's own son,
Yes, He was the Holy One.
And His name was Jesus.

Jesus was the King of Kings,
But He had no purple things.
Royal robe—no, and no rings—
Just His friends and family.

Then there came a purple day.
Clouds, they turned amethyst-gray.
Crowds, they sent this King away—
Crucified sweet Jesus.

Three days hence He rose again
To free you and me from sin.
Evil loses and we win
If we follow Jesus."

Pippa looked in Mother's eyes,
Sorry for the purple prize
That had filled her heart with lies,
Robbing her of real love.

Pippa

That night Pippa's heart was changed.
Everything was rearranged.

Purple love—
it seemed so strange.
For she had met *Real Love*.

This was Pippa's bedtime prayer,
"Lord, replace the purple bear.
Fill me with your love to share.
I believe in Jesus."

Pippa now loves people more
Than the purple in each store.
Her heart's eyes no longer war
With this wondrous color.

And Pippa enjoys each hue,

Yellow,

black,

brown,

green,

and blue,

Orange bikes, red yo-yos, too—
The girl who loved purple.

About the Author

Priscilla Doremus is a married mother of two who currently lives in Sugar Land, Texas. She has enjoyed writing from the time she was just a young child, and is passionate about writing meaningful works in every genre. She is a graduate of Baylor University, and often patterns certain aspects of her characters after friends and family members. In her spare time, Priscilla enjoys baking chocolate chip cookies and spending time with family and friends. For more information about the author, please visit her blog at priscilladoremus.com.

About the Illustrator

Ariane Elsammak offers high quality humorous & whimsical illustrations for many different fields of work from children's books and magazines to designs for apparel. She creates quality illustrations in both traditional & digital formats in a timely manner. She listens and works closely with her clients to reach a high standard of excellence. Ariane studied editorial and children's book illustration at the School of Visual Arts in New York City and the DuCret School of Art in New Jersey. Visit her site at artbyari.com.